RIVERDALE

He Loves Me, She Loves Me Not

Riverdale's Guide to Crushes, Heartbreaks, and True Romance

by **Jenne Simon**

Scholastic Inc.

Contents

Addicted to Love

They say romance is dead. But in the fair town of Riverdale, not only is it alive and well, it comes with a milk shake and a side of fries. Whether you're looking for some *flirty fun* on a Friday night or longing for a *forever love*, you've come to the right place. The students of Riverdale High have hooked up with hotties, been burned by the sizzle of forbidden romance, and fallen for their soul mates. And they're here to tell you everything they know about relationships: the good, the bad, and the totally weird.

How did a blue-collar babe like Archie Andrews ever get together with Park Avenue princess Veronica Lodge? *Instant chemistry, baby*. He's the Jay to her Bey, and they wouldn't have it any other way. Betty Cooper and Jughead Jones (*Bughead*, to all you shippers) have survived serial killers, gang wars, and overprotective parents because she sees the beauty in his darkness and he sees the darkness in her beauty.

Just remember: Relationships aren't all diners, drive-ins, and date nights. Riverdale is the capital of complications, and any couple in town can tell you that the path to love can be more twisted than a Blossom family reunion. But as Archie says, "You can't go through life trying not to get hurt." So get ready to lay your heart bare, and you just might have a chance at finding *the big L*.

6

Chapter 1

CRUSHING IT

Crushing It

Nothing is as exciting as a crush. Or as nauseating. From stolen glances to private fantasies, swiping right to meeting cute, infatuation can be a full-time job.

THE BLUE & GOLD

DEAR RONNIE

Relationship advice from some-one who's been there, done that
by Veronica Lodge

Dear Ronnie,

I've got a major crush on a redheaded bombshell who is way out of my league. She's rich—like, mega-owns-half-the-county rich—and is used to getting whatever she wants. I'm from the wrong side of the tracks. And even though she doesn't seem to care, I know her mother disapproves of me. Should I try to get the girl anyway?

—Topaz in the Rough

Dear Topaz,

You say this girl is used to getting what she wants? Well, she obviously wants you. So what if Mommy Dearest doesn't like it. She's not the one you want to date, anyway. I say, go for it!

And while we're on the subject of what you want, no need to be so thirsty. Don't let that niggling little voice inside your head convince you that money makes a person worthy of love. Trust me, my parents have cash for days, and we aren't exactly functional. Money can buy Prada and Porsches, but never kindness.

XO,
Ronnie

Dear Ronnie,

I'm totally hung up on a sweet, big, moose of a guy. I know he likes me, too—he's super sweet when we're alone. But he'll only see me on the DL, and refuses to make our relationship public. He's totally my type, but he's got more demons than *The Exorcist*. Should I try to tame this animal or release him back into the wild?

—His Dirty Little Secret

Dear HDLS,

Sneaking around can be exciting. But if it's a real relationship you're after, it's time to put this beast out of his misery. You deserve a man who will shout how he feels about you from the mountaintops.

This guy obviously isn't in touch with who he is or what he wants. He only cares about what people think. So ignore the animal attraction, and stay away . . . at least until he grows some cojones, and can admit who he is and what he wants.

XO,
Ronnie

For more relationship advice, please contact Dear Ronnie on Twitter or Instagram, or email dear-ronnie@riverdalehigh.edu.

What's Your Type?

Are you drawn to sensitive artists? Do take-charge personalities make you swoon? Or do you think the brain is the sexiest organ around? Discover the type you're most likely to crush on with this handy quiz.

1. What is your favorite kind of music?

A. Upbeat pop songs that are easy to dance to.

B. Award winners only. If it hasn't won a Grammy, you aren't here for it.

C. Emo all the way. You like your music moody and passionate.

D. Original compositions by singer-songwriters with something to say.

2. How do you feel about group dates?

A. The more the merrier. Tailgating is so much fun in a pack.

B. As long as someone brings the drama, you're happy to go along.

C. Anyone you'd want to date wouldn't be caught dead in a crowd.

D. You'd prefer to fly solo with that special someone.

3. What's your idea of a perfect Saturday night?

A. A romantic movie at the Bijou, followed by burgers at Pop's. Good clean fun.

B. Creating some chaos . . . just for kicks. You can't help being a bombshell.

C. Contemplating the meaning of life down by Sweetwater River.

D. Steaming up the windows of your classic car with that special someone.

4.

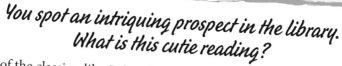

You spot an intriguing prospect in the library. What is this cutie reading?

A. One of the classics, like *Beloved* or *American Psycho*.

B. A self-help book: *The Secret* or *How to Win Friends and Influence People*.

C. Something cerebral—and cynical—by Kurt Vonnegut or Emily Dickinson.

D. *The Artist's Way*. Their creativity and drive can't be contained.

5.

What is the first thing you notice about a person?

A. A friendly smile that can light up a room.

B. Attitude—a pretty face may be nice, but confidence is sexy.

C. Eyes are the windows to the soul. You like a pair with some intelligence behind them.

D. The way they use their hands to strum a guitar, paint a picture, and so much more.

6.

On Halloween, you spot a babe whose costume is no trick, all treat. What are they dressed as?

A. An astronaut or sexy kitten. Traditional doesn't have to mean boring.

B. Royalty—you bow down before those who command respect.

C. Themselves—you prefer someone who is confident in their own skin.

D. Elvis or Marilyn. You have a thing for tortured performers.

Quiz Results

Mostly As

The Sweetheart

You are attracted to the wholesome good looks and sweet-as-apple-pie personalities of darlings like Betty Cooper or Kevin Keller. But while you think you know exactly what you're getting with these all-American sweethearts, everyone has a dark side . . .

Mostly Bs

The Ego

You can't resist someone with sass and class who speaks their mind, like Cheryl Blossom or Reggie Mantle. They're a little full of themselves? *Quelle* surprise. These big-headed baes are used to demanding attention—and total devotion. Are you prepared to kiss their feet?

Mostly Cs

The Loner

You're drawn to independent-minded thinkers who forge their own paths, like Jughead Jones or Ethel Muggs. Sure, they can spend too much time thinking about the harsh, grim realities of the world. But dig a little deeper and you'll find fiery passions behind their nerdy armor.

Mostly Ds

The Artist

You fall for sensitive, creative types who bare their souls through their art, like Archie Andrews or Josie McCoy. But they're no starving artists. They have ambition and drive to show the world how they feel about everything from love and romance to injustice and prejudice.

MASH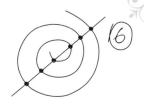

LIVES IN

~~New York City~~
~~Paris~~
~~Los Angeles~~
(Riverdale)

DRIVES

(Volvo)
~~Prius~~
~~Tesla~~
~~Bus Pass~~

JOBS

~~Politician~~
(Journalist)
~~1st Grade Teacher~~
~~Stay at Home Mom~~

SPOUSE

(Jughead)
~~Archie~~
~~Chuck Clayton~~
~~None~~

KIDS

~~0~~
~~1~~
(2)
~~6~~

SATISFACTION

(Dark, Twisted Bliss)
~~Bored but Content~~
~~Miserable~~
~~Dreams Come True~~

So Juggie and I are going to live happily
ever after in Riverdale? I'll take it!

To Flirt, or Not to Flirt

When you have your eye on someone special, it can be as exciting—and terrifying—as a roller coaster ride. The rules of attraction are complicated. If you're too bold, you risk looking #desperate. Too chill? Your crush won't even notice you. But whether you're falling hard or hardly falling, you need a solid seduction strategy to win the game of love. Which one is right for you?

Strategy 1

Friends First

Betty believes in buddying up to the object of her affection. But don't get stuck in the Friend Zone, like she did with Archie. It takes longing glances, inside jokes, and common interests (a little B&E by moonlight, anyone?) to turn a boy friend into a boyfriend.

Just ask Jughead!

The Art of Flirtation

Veronica knows that any flirtationship begins with a tease of the senses. So dress to impress. Tell dirty jokes. Wear an alluring scent. Get a little touchy-feely. And smile, for the love of Chris Hemsworth. When your crush sees you living it up, you'll be totally irresistible.

Go Big or Go Home

Cheryl prefers the direct approach. People may think you're a little cuckoo for Cocoa Puffs, but there's no point in dancing around your desires . . . unless, of course, you're into that. So don't wait for someone to ask you out. Be a bombshell and let your feelings explode.

19

Chapter 2

THE DATING GAME

CHERYL BLOSSOM'S
GUIDE TO DATING

Listen up fives,
a ten is speaking.

Dating is a double-edged sword. Sure, it's nice to have a hot honey on your arm on a Saturday night. But if you don't know what you're doing, your evening can go from *True Romance* to *Night of the Living Dead* in an instant.

As a lifelong member of Riverdale royalty, Cheryl Blossom knows what it means to be treated like a queen. So here are a few of her top tips to make your next date night unforgettable.

Get The Look

Before a big date, always make sure you're dressed and groomed appropriately. First impressions are everything, after all. This cherry bombshell swears that wearing designer duds in your signature power color is sure to make you feel ready to slay.

Fiercely Formal

figure
flattering

fur
gloves

clutch
accessory

sky-high
heels

Ice Princess Chic

red riding
hood

diva cape

Biker Babe

exclusive
jacket

SOUTH SIDE
S
SERPENTS

luxe
leather

badass
boots

25

Paint the Town

What you do on a date is almost as important as what you wear. If you bore Cheryl, she's outie, all right?

Fine Dining

Going to dinner is the obvious choice, but remember: Blossoms are strictly gourmet. Skip the diner and let your honey get to know you over some candle mood lighting instead.

Lights! Camera! Action!

Movies and date night go together like Dolce & Gabbana. Sure, you may not be able to talk much, but sitting close together in the dark is a great way to test your chemistry. If the heat between you melts your Milk Duds, you know sparks are flying.

Raise a Glass

Every truly special night out ends with a visit to a lavish lounge like La Bonne Nuit, Riverdale's only retro speakeasy. Sip a mocktail, take in the soulful stylings of resident chanteuse Josephine McCoy, and dance under twinkling lights until the sun comes up.

Say Goodnight

When the evening comes to an end, you have a big choice to make: to kiss, or not to kiss. Is your date Prince or Princess Charming, or just a frog you're ready to ditch?

Reasons to Kiss

- ♥ tells witty jokes
- ♥ entertaining
- ♥ great hair
- ♥ treats you like a queen
- ♥ you're into it

Reasons to Diss

- ✕ tells boring stories
- ✕ condescending
- ✕ bad breath
- ✕ treats you like a trophy
- ✕ you're not feeling it

THE BLUE & GOLD

WEEKLY NEWSPAPER OF RIVERDALE HIGH

DEAR RONNIE

**Relationship advice from some-
one who's been there, done that**
by Veronica Lodge

Dear Ronnie,

My girlfriend is the sweetest girl in Riverdale, but we're total opposites. She's a straight-A student, a cheerleader. And the truth is, I'm weird. I don't fit in, and I don't *want* to fit in. I'm a damaged outsider who only feels comfortable alone or among the gang of outlaws I ride with. I love her, but I don't want her to try to change me. Are we on borrowed time?

—The Serpent King

Dear Serpent King,

You're making an awful lot of assumptions about this girlfriend of yours. Who says she wants you to change? Have you asked her? Besides, she may be a little conventional to the outside world, but if she's as amazing as you say, surely she has layers.

That's the thing about human

beings—we contain multitudes. You like solitude *and* hanging with your motorhead family, right? Isn't she allowed to be more than just the perfect girl next door? If you want your love to last, she's not the one who needs to be open-minded—you are.

XO,
Ronnie

Dear Ronnie,

I admit it: I've always been a player. And when it comes to kissing and telling, I don't have the best track record. Now my past is ruining my future. I've fallen for a girl with the voice of an angel who wants nothing to do with me. How can I get her to see that I've changed?

—Reformed Ladies' Man

Dear RLM,

How do you show someone you've changed? *By changing.* That means no more hard partying or locker room bragging. Lying about giving a girl a sticky maple might damage her reputation, but it also shreds yours. And any consequences you suffer because of it are well deserved IMO. All you can do is hope that your dream girl notices the new you and wants to give you a second chance.

XO,
Ronnie

For more relationship advice, please contact Dear Ronnie on Twitter or Instagram, or email dear-ronnie@riverdalehigh.edu.

We've had this date with each other from the very beginning, Archiekins.

AQUARIUS
January 20–February 18

PISCES
February 19–March 20

ARIES
March 21–April 19

TAURUS
April 20–May 20

GEMINI
May 21–June 20

CANCER
June 21–July 22

LEO
July 23–August 22

VIRGO
August 23–September 22

LIBRA
September 23–October 22

SCORPIO
October 23–November 21

SAGITTARIUS
November 22–December 21

CAPRICORN
December 22–January 19

What's Your Sign?

In Riverdale, romance is written in the stars. Are you and
your sweetest steady as astrologically compatible as Betty and
Jughead? Or are you destined to be single forever? We've looked
to the heavens and plotted a course for love. What does your
horoscope have in store?

Like Toni Topaz, *aquariuses* are free spirits who guard their independence fiercely. But underneath that laid-back exterior beats the heart of a serpent who mates for life. You'll only settle for a soul mate who's also your best friend.

Pisces are like Polly Cooper—they love to be in love. Romance can be as all-consuming and addictive as a day at the Farm. But living with your honey in a magical fantasy world means you can have a hard time accepting reality.

If you're an *aries*, you're a Big Man on Campus who's not into being suffocated or controlled, just like Reggie Mantle. You love both giving and receiving attention. And while you like to play the field, when you find that special someone, you go all in.

Taurus signs are old-fashioned like Kevin Keller when it comes to love. You want a stable partner who's affectionate and loyal. But you can be bullheaded, which can make it hard to figure out when it's time to let bad love go.

Like Chuck Clayton, *geminis* like to play games. One minute you're sending flirty texts, the next you're talking trash. But after the dramatic will-they-or-won't-they beginnings of a seduction, you're easily bored. You'd much rather have a fling than the real thing.

Cancers are sensitive and sentimental, intuitive and moody, like Betty Cooper. You'd rather spend a Saturday cozying up on the couch than hitting the town. But when someone you care about needs you, you'll put yourself in danger to defend your love.

Like Cheryl Blossom, *leos* are proud, flamboyant, and incredibly dramatic. You want the whole world to bow down at your feet—only head cases would dare cross you. Your perfect match is someone who'll spoil you like crazy *and* keep your ego in check.

Virgos are perfectionists, just like Josie McCoy. It's hard for anyone to meet your high standards. You'd rather be alone than settle for so-so suitors. But if you want forever love, you'll need to sing a different tune and accept that everyone has flaws.

Like Jughead Jones, *libras* are idealists who look for stability in a soul mate. You believe in telling the truth and playing fair. But sometimes you can be too self-sacrificing. Your perfect partner will make sure you aren't always taking one for the team.

Scorpios are like Moose Mason: mysterious. You know how to keep a secret, and you have many you'll take to the grave. Only those lucky enough to make it past your tough defenses get a glimpse of your intensely passionate nature.

If you're a *sagittarius*, you're like Archie Andrews—a people pleaser who changes to suit the one you're with. You can write sensitive love songs, charm the strictest parents, and even bare-knuckle it to protect the one you care about most.

Like Veronica Lodge, *capricorns* approach love as serious business. Calculating and stubborn, you don't play around when it comes to matters of the heart. You know who you want and you aren't afraid to go get them—even if it means crossing your family.

DATING: SERPENT STYLE

If picnics by Sweetwater River or a night at the Twilight Drive-In sound like a snoozefest, these tips from the Southside's resident biker gang might help spice up your Saturday night.

* A **SERPENT** NEVER SHEDS HIS SKIN. MEANING? WEAR YOUR BEST LEATHER.

* IF YOU WANT TO GET CLOSE, SKIP THE CAR AND PICK UP YOUR DATE ON A **HARLEY.**

* DIVE BARS LIKE THE **WHYTE WYRM** ARE A GREAT PLACE TO GET TO KNOW SOMEONE . . . AS LONG AS YOU KEEP YOUR EYES ON YOUR OWN TABLE.

* FEELING COMPETITIVE? SHOOT SOME POOL. **WINNER** GETS A KISS.

* FOCUS ON YOUR DATE. DON'T PICK A FIGHT WITH A **PREPPY NORTHSIDER** OR DRUGGED-OUT **GHOULIE.**

* IN **UNITY,** THERE IS STRENGTH. IF YOUR HEART GETS BUSTED, DROWN YOUR SORROWS WITH A FRIEND.

Chapter 3

GETTING
ROMANTIC

39

Getting Romantic

Once you've found that special someone, it's the sexy secrets, stolen glances, and sweet surprises that keep the chemistry sizzling.

SETTING THE MOOD
WITH REGGIE MANTLE

When a high-octane hottie gives you a look that says they're down to Netflix and chill, you want an amorous atmosphere that's sure to sizzle. Think you're too manly for romance? In the Book of Reg, caring enough to make things sweet for that special someone makes you a top-tier, loyal badass.

Here's how:

• Dim the lights, but don't go full dark. You're going for sighs, not snores.

• Light candles—you can't mess with this classic move.

• Pamper your honey. You can never go wrong with chocolate and massages.

• R.E.S.P.E.C.T. Find out what it means to . . . your partner.

• Put on soft music. Nothin' says lovin' like a sweet melody.

JOSIE'S
SMOOTHEST SLOW JAMS:
A ROMANTIC PLAYLIST

"Fever" by Peggy Lee * "Filthy" by Justin Timberlake * "Shape of You" by Ed Sheeran * "Summer" by The Carters * "Kiss" by Prince * "Faded Love" by Tinashe featuring Future * "Call Out My Name" by The Weeknd * "Beg" by Jack & Jack * "Make Me Feel" by Janelle Monáe * "Let Me" by Zayn * "Let's Get It On" by Marvin Gaye * "I Feel Love" by Donna Summer * "Nice & Slow" by Usher * "Skin" by Rihanna * "Burning Desire" by Lana Del Rey

Love Nests

Every good fling needs a cozy little hideaway where your love can bloom. Kevin Keller has had his share of adventure, so he knows all the best spots for hookups, hangouts, and whispering sweet nothings in your bae's ear.

In the Wild

Fresh air, moonlight, and birdsong add an invigorating rush to clandestine get-togethers. But if your baby likes to hang in the great outdoors, just make sure to pick the pine needles from your hair before you head back to civilization.

In the Closet

No, literally in the janitor's closet at school. Hiding who you are from the world never works. But hiding away when you want to share a steamy moment? Any empty classroom or locked office will do.

In Secret

Everyone knows that three is a crowd. So the best places to keep a relationship private are the ones no one ever visits. A derelict bunker or abandoned shack make for great rendezvous. No DO NOT DISTURB sign necessary.

The Dark Side of Love

Sometimes even the sweetest romances need a little mystery to keep things interesting. And no one knows this better than Riverdale's very own Betty Cooper. This girl next door has a dark side that would put Darth Vader to shame. Spice up your love life with some of Dark Betty's boldest moves.

Play Dress Up

Feeling shy? Role-play your way to confidence. A cheeky wig and wardrobe can help you invent a character who's a little more daring and not afraid to take risks.

Dance All Night

Betty doesn't believe in the old adage "Dance like no one's watching." She slithered her way into the Southside Serpents with a sexy initiation dance. All eyes were on her—including those of her forever love, Jughead.

Create Some Chaos

Every once in a while, Betty takes a page from Cheryl Blossom's book and does the unexpected. So kiss a stranger. Throw a party. Tell your crush how you really feel. And regret nothing.

Recommended Reading

If the brain is the sexiest part of the body, a romantic novel can definitely put you in the mood. Here are a few suggestions of books that will sweep you off your feet.

Beloved by Toni Morrison

Call Me By Your Name by André Aciman

Me Before You by Jojo Moyes

Lady Chatterley's Lover by D. H. Lawrence

Outlander by Diana Gabaldon

Love in the Time of Cholera
by Gabriel García Márquez

The Time Traveler's Wife
by Audrey Niffenegger

To All the Boys I've Loved Before
by Jenny Han

Pride and Prejudice by Jane Austen

The Notebook by Nicholas Sparks

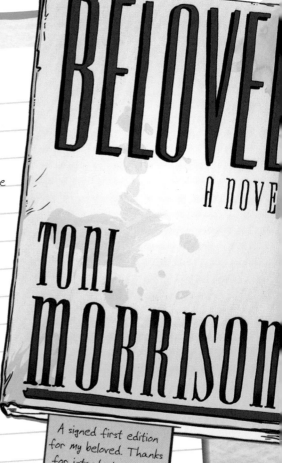

BELOVED

A NOVE

TONI
MORRISON

A signed first edition
for my beloved. Thanks
for introducing me to
your favorite writer.
Love, Jug

Flower Power

The Blossoms of Riverdale don't have any trouble saying what's on their mind. But for the less loquacious among us, knowing the secret language of flowers can let you express how you truly feel. And Cheryl's broken down the meaning behind each of these beautiful bouquets.

Yellow Roses mean you're color-blind.

Daisies are for purity and innocence. Boring!

Purple hyacinths say, "Please forgive me." But expensive jewelry says it better.

Pink carnations technically say, "I'll never forget you." But they also say, "I'm cheap."

Sweet peas are the flowers of endings and good-byes. Guess that's why Jughead's greaser buddy is always getting the kiss-off.

Red roses mean love and respect. They're the only flower worth accepting.

Chapter 4

LOVE HURTS

Love Hurts

Let's face it: Not every romance ends happily ever after. Unrequited love, hurt feelings, and heartbreak can't always be avoided. And when love sours, only the truly emo survive.

"The Song That Everyone Sings"

Written and performed by Archie Andrews

Tales of the old,
Of the secrets we hold.
I want to be well,
I'm lucky to even feel
Love at all.

Words run like a race,
And maybe I spoke too late.
You try and erase,
Every memory, every shape,
But I host them in place.

Tales of the old,
Of the secrets we hold.
I want to be well,
And maybe I'll never feel
Love at all.

It's the song that everyone sings.
It's the song that everyone sings.
It's the song that everyone sings.

Where have I gone?
And where have you gone?

Take me back to summertime,
Endless love, and endless wine.
I want you.
I want you.
Take me back to summertime,
Endless love, and endless wine.
I want you.
I want you.

Writing the Pain Away

Sometimes the only remedy for a broken heart is to wallow in a truly sad song. Or, when all else fails and your heart is laid bare, journal your way through the pain.

Tuesday, October 12th

In Riverdale, the Black Hood isn't the only one who wears a mask. But every so often, the mask slips and our true selves are laid bare for all the world to see. So we scramble to put it back on, like a kid in a cheap Halloween costume, but it's too late. People have already seen what's underneath. And it's terrifying.

—Jughead Jones

DEAR RONNIE

Relationship advice from someone who's been there, done that

by Veronica Lodge

Dear Ronnie,

My boyfriend and I used to have tons in common—we're both smart, keep to ourselves, and are obsessed with playing Gryphons and Gargoyles. He was my Hellcaster, and I was his Princess. But he betrayed me and finished our game with someone else. Should I bottle up my heartbreak or let my feelings rage?

—Damsel in Distress

Dear Damsel,

I'm so sorry you're in pain. Rejection hurts more than a full-sleeve tattoo, and sometimes it can even feel as permanent. But keeping your emotions locked up inside will only get you a quick ticket to Crazytown. You have to channel your feelings into something productive. Control your anger and sadness or they'll control you. Lashing out doesn't help, either. Try laying off the fantasy role-playing for a while, and appreciate all the good things you have going on IRL. You'll find a way to slay your dragons, one by one.

XO,
Ronnie

Dear Ronnie,

I'm ambitious to a fault. Yet last summer, I threw my focus out the window for a fling with a bad boy. When we got together, I warned him that our hookup came with an expiration date. Now he wants more, but I can't afford to be distracted by a tall, cool drink of Sweetwater. Is dumping him the right call?

—Curiosity Killed the Pussycat

Dear Pussycat,

Newsflash: Banning something only makes it more interesting. If you're having a good time together, what's the harm? Expiration dates are for sour milk and trendy accessories, not romance. *But* if your career is truly your top priority, put the fling on ice. Sure, it's hard to break up when your feelings haven't cooled. But you don't make *Fibe*'s "20 Under 20" by fooling around at pool parties or sneaking off for illicit rendezvous.

XO,
Ronnie

For more relationship advice, please contact Dear Ronnie on Twitter or Instagram, or email dear-ronnie@riverdalehigh.edu.

Bad Romance

Some romance is doomed from the start. But if you don't want to be one of the truly tragic, follow these Riverdale dating don'ts.

DON'T put your drink down at a party, especially if your date seems too good to be true. Roofies don't come with a warning.

DON'T try to elope without telling anyo... Romeo and Juliet may seem like the ideal du... but their romance ended badly.

DON'T date a teacher. As if the age gap weren't problematic enough, the power dynamic is uncomfortable ... and illegal.

DON'T work for your girlfriend's father. Even if she's a daddy's girl, they'll butt heads and you'll be stuck in the middle.

DON'T sneak around with someone who's already spoken for. It's classless and gross. Plus, you'll be the prime suspect if something sinister happens.

DON'T go cruising in the woods by your lonesome. You never know what danger... may be lurking in the shadows.

The End of Love

by Ethel Muggs

Roses are dead.

My lips are blue.

I never thought that

I'd bury you.

Trapped in a role

That leaves no way out,

Never believing

My fear and my doubt.

My mouth was sewn closed,

But that's true no longer.

And with the King's guidance

I grow ever stronger.

Now that you've left me

A chalice to raise,

I will be faithful

The rest of my days.

Revenge

When someone does you wrong, you have two choices: You can take the high road, or you can burn everything to the ground. We all know which option Cheryl Blossom chooses. The High Priestess of Payback has lots of creative suggestions for showing cheaters, chokers, and frenemies exactly who they're messing with.

Laundry Time

Airing an ex's dirty laundry isn't fair, but it sure is fun. So gossip with a bigmouth, play a party game like Secrets and Sins, or even take out an ad in the *Blue & Gold* to make sure everyone knows about the bad seed you used to date.

Texting Turnaround

If a cheater wounds your pride, clap back with a stunt that is sure to show them the true meaning of humiliation. Snag their phone and start swapping numbers. When they text their side piece, and get an angry reply from their boss instead, you've won.

Yard Sale

The expensive headphones she left in your bedroom? The promise ring he said meant you'd be together forever? The one-of-a-kind sneakers you bought for his birthday? Finders keepers is the law of the land after a breakup. So sell the things they left behind and use the profits to spoil yourself.

Moving On

Whether you're suffering the sting of unrequited love or just moving in different directions with your longtime boo, breaking up bites the big one. It can make you feel more unwanted than a pimple on prom night, and moving on is never easy. Here are a few of the Riverdale crew's surefire cures for a broken heart.

Cry It Out

Sometimes screaming into your pillow is the best way to purge your pain and, in the immortal words of Taylor Swift, shake it off. So cry on a friend's shoulder, burn your ex in effigy, and listen to sad songs on repeat—anything to get your feelings out.

Treat Yourself

Self-care isn't optional. This is never more true than when you're feeling vulnerable after a breakup. So binge on ice cream, plan a spa day with your BFF, or go on an exotic vacation. You deserve a little luxury, and taking care of yourself is the quickest way to inspire your ex's jealousy and regret.

Go Fishing

There are millions of fish in the sea, and now's the time to play catch and release. Rebound all over town, but keep it casual. You might not be ready to dive headfirst into a new relationship, but that doesn't mean you can't dip your toes in the water.

Give It Time

You can't hurry love, and you can't underestimate how long it will take you to get over it. Betty moved on from her crush on Archie, but it took more than playing *True Detective* with Jughead to get her there. It took time.

64

Chapter 5

THE REAL DEAL

The Real Deal

True love is like a good steak. Hot. Rare. Nourishing. Finding it is nothing short of a miracle. So when you do find it, don't let it go. Grab that ginger bull by the horns and hang on for dear life!

Will Your Love Last?

Not every romance is built for the long haul. But how do you know if it's true love or just a passing infatuation? Take this quiz to find out if your relationship is right for a reason, a season, or a lifetime.

1. *It's your birthday, and even though you were hoping for a quiet night in, bae throws you a surprise party. How do you feel?*

A. Happy—getting all the people you care about together was so thoughtful!

B. Elated—you LOVE surprises. Your honey knows you better than you know yourself.

C. Annoyed—shouldn't your birthday be about what you actually want?

2. *You find out your steady has been keeping a gigantic secret from you. How do you react?*

A. Grill them for hours, and use it as ammunition for future fights.

B. Try to stay open-minded, and talk about why they were holding back.

C. Ignore it. If they didn't think it was important, why should you?

3.

You and your partner are pulled apart by circumstances outside of your control. How you deal with long distance love?

A. Pen a love letter every day and visit on weekends so they know you care.

B. Ghost their texts and avoid making plans. Absence makes the heart grow fonder.

C. Lie, steal, and cheat—whatever it takes to get them back.

4.

It's time to meet the parents. What's your best-case scenario?

A. They like you. And you and your partner remain a team they can't divide.

B. They love you. You know how to wrap adults around your finger.

C. They hate you. Now you get out of all family reunions and holiday obligations.

5.

How does your girlfriend or boyfriend comfort you when you're feeling down in the dumps?

A. They suggest something crazy like running away together.

B. They listen to your fears without judgment.

C. They tell you jokes to lighten the mood and make you smile.

Quiz Results

Check your answers against this key and add up your point total to find out whether your relationship is going nowhere or going the distance.

Q1: a=2, b=1, c=0

Q2: a=0, b=2, c=1

Q3: a=1, b=0, c=2

Q4: a=2, b=1, c=0

Q5: a=0, b=2, c=1

0–3 points

Doomed
to Fail

You may love his bad reputation or her magnetic charm, but true love needs more than animal attraction to flourish. If you can't occasionally put the relationship ahead of your own needs, your love will never survive. Just look at Alice and FP . . .

4–7 points

Just Right
for Right Now

You two have a lot in common. But that doesn't mean you'll always be moving in the same direction. Enjoy your time together, and pay attention to the heart warmers and deal breakers in your relationship. When your soul mate comes along, you'll be ready.

8–10 points

Forever
Isn't Long Enough

Your love has staying power. You know each other's strengths and flaws, and like Betty and Jughead, you've mastered the art of communication. Lasting romance means knowing when to talk your problems out and when to spring into action on your partner's behalf.

EPIC ENDGAMES

Like Varchie, you may think you know the meaning of forever. But the real deal doesn't come along very often. Study these famously devoted duos to discover the secret to lasting love.

Marc Antony and Cleopatra

They shared passion, politics, and a flair for the dramatic. Their affair might have ended with a cobra bite, but their love story lives on.

Queen Victoria and Prince Albert

When Prince Albert died, Queen Victoria went into mourning and wore only black for the next forty years.

Clyde Barrow and Bonnie Parker

Cold-blooded killers who lied together, loved together, and died together. The ultimate partners in crime.

Gertrude Stein and Alice B. Toklas

Their Parisian apartment was the heart of the literary and art scene, but it was their quiet devotion that really inspired awe.

Michelle and Barack Obama

Theirs is a rare political union that has nothing to do with power or money and everything to do with love and respect.

Dear Betty,

You are the beat of my heart, the Sherlock to my Watson. Most people think I'm just some moody, serial killer fanboy freak, too busy writing manifestos to pay attention to other humans. But you've always seen what's going on beneath this ridiculous hat of mine. I've spent my life living in the darkness, but you are my light. Have I ever told you how lucky I am to know you?

Sometimes I wish we could just hop on my motorcycle and leave Riverdale. Go someplace where there is no Northside or Southside. No creepy cults or obsessive games. No murders to investigate. Somewhere where the only thing we'd have to think about is the sun on our faces and the wind at our backs.

But I know we're the only ones who can figure out what's going on in this messed-up, Twin Peaks–reboot town of ours. Together, there's no way the darkness can beat us. I love you, Betty Cooper.

Yours forever,
Jug

15 SIGNS YOU'RE A POWER COUPLE

by Cheryl Blossom and Toni Topaz

1. You don't keep secrets. Spilling the tea isn't risky when you *trust* each other.

2. You're *supportive* in any situation. Trolls beware.

3. The *attraction* is real. You think your honey is pure fire.

4. When you talk about your partner, you can't resist the *humblebrag*.

5. You *fight fair*. No below-the-belt digs. No clapping back.

6. You *learn* from your mistakes and move on.

7. You're *friends* first.

8. You *compromise*, no matter the sitch.

9. You *communicate* your needs without getting too salty.

11. When you *hit the town*, your looks break the internet. Everyone wants to hang in your orbit.

10. You try new things *together*.

12. You don't try to *change* each other.

13. You have common interests. Drag racing and binge-watching *Game of Thrones* are both more *fun à deux*.

14. You both get some *alone time*. Codependence is cancelled.

15. You help each other *dream big*.

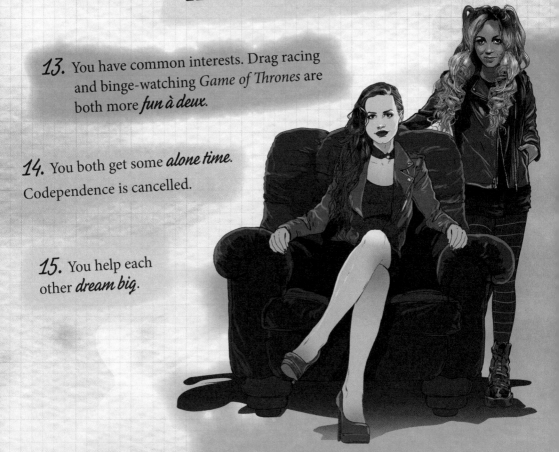

THE PERFECT KISS

Veronica had to kiss a lot of frogs before she found her Prince Archiekins. And not all lip-locks are created equally. So before you pucker up, get the skinny on the perfect smooch.

Make sure the kiss is wanted. Consent is nonnegotiable.

Anticipation is everything. Make 'em beg for it.

A kiss isn't all in the lips. Try adding a touch to the cheek or hair.

Avoid sticky lip gloss. Instead, go for a deep stain that won't rub off.

Don't kiss anyone whose oral hygiene leaves anything to be desired.

Slow down. A good kiss is a marathon, not a sprint.

A little nibble can be exciting, but be gentle.

Happy Anniversary

Whether you're counting the days, marking the months, or celebrating years of coupled bliss, spoiling your sweetheart with a meaningful anniversary present can show them how much they mean to you. Go old-school and get inspired by these traditional-themed offerings.

1st Anniversary—Paper For your first big celebration, give your partner the gift of words, like a love letter or a first edition of her favorite book.

2nd Anniversary—Cotton Soft hearts deserve soft presents: a painted canvas portrait for her or a boxing bag for him to practice his best bare-knuckle moves.

3rd Anniversary—Leather Sometimes tough love keeps a couple together. A motorcycle jacket and studded boots are the ultimate symbol of romantic strength.

4th Anniversary—Fruit Commemorate the fruits of your relationship by ordering a strawberry malt or turning lemons into lemonade—just be sure to ask for two straws.

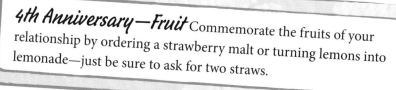

5th Anniversary—Wood Get back to nature with a canoe to paddle down Sweetwater River. Or sweeten things up with a bottle of Blossom maple syrup.

"I Got You"

Music and Lyrics by Archie Andrews and Valerie Brown

I get a little bit overwhelmed,
But I find you when I need you most.
You are the compass that I've always held
'Cause around you I can be myself.

I'm trying, oh, I'm turning the page.
We're animals breaking out of our cage.
There's nobody, no one, nowhere who gets me like you do.
And I know it ain't gonna change.
You always pull me through.
We're as wild as we can be.
I got you and you got me.
I got you. You got me.

We grew tall in the same small town,
Stealing shopping carts that we'd race around.
Late at night, looking at the stars,
Carrying moonbeams home in our mason jars.

I'm ready now, I'm turning the page.
We're animals breaking out of our cage.
There's nobody, no one, nowhere who gets me like you do.

And I know it ain't gonna change.
You always pull me through.
We're as wild as we can be.
I got you and you got me.
I got you. You got me.

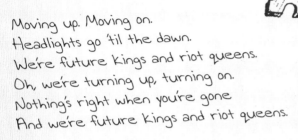

Moving up. Moving on.
Headlights go 'til the dawn.
We're future kings and riot queens.
Oh, we're turning up, turning on.
Nothing's right when you're gone
And we're future kings and riot queens.

And nobody, no one, nowhere
Nobody, no one, nowhere
And I know it ain't gonna change.

There's nobody, no one, nowhere who gets me like you do.
And I know it ain't gonna change.
You always pull me through.
We're as wild as we can be.
I got you and you got me.
I got you. You got me.
I got you. You got me.

Ronnie,
This song existed before we were
a thing, but somehow it's still
about you. I love you.
—Archie